This book
belongs to

_____

ON MY WAY WITH SESAME STREET

Volume 4

Animals, Animals

Featuring Jim Henson's Sesame Street Muppets

Children's Television Workshop/Funk & Wagnalls

Authors

Liza Alexander
B.G. Ford
Michaela Muntean
Rae Paige

Illustrators

Tom Cooke
Tom Leigh
Jean Zallinger

Photos courtesy of ANIMALS ANIMALS, THE BETTMANN ARCHIVE and PHOTO RESEARCHERS, INC.

0-8343-0078-8

A Parents' Guide to ANIMALS, ANIMALS

Children can learn a lot from animals. Caring for pets helps teach children empathy and acceptance of responsibility. Learning about animals' needs for food, sleep and shelter is a good way to introduce natural science.

Many children are first fascinated by farm animals and the sounds they make. Baby animals have a particular appeal. So ''Baby Animals on the Farm,'' introduced by lovable, furry old Grover, is guaranteed to delight! Later in the book, Grover displays photographs of baby animals who live on the farm, in the forest and in the jungle.

Children can learn about bats from the Count and cats from Herry Monster and try to answer ''Oscar's Yucchy Questions.'' Cookie Monster, of course, wants to know ''What's for Dinner?'' and learns what different animals eat.

In ''Big Bird's Trip to the Zoo,'' children meet lions, tigers, bears and a bird as tall as Big Bird!

From under the sea to the depths of the jungle, this book will give your child an excellent introduction to ANIMALS, ANIMALS and their world.

The Editors
SESAME STREET BOOKS

Baby Animals on the Farm

"Hello, everybodee! It is I, Grover. Would you like to meet some cute and fuzzy baby animals? Of course you would! Lots have just been born on the farm because it is spring! The baby animals will have the warm summer to grow big and strong before winter comes. Come along, now!"

"Greetings, Grover!" said the Count. "Meet six wonderful kittens!"

"Hello, Count," said Grover. "Hello, little kitties. You are very cute and furry, but you are not blue!"

"Let's count all the kitties!" said the Count. "One calico kitten. Two striped kittens. Two black kittens with mittens. There should be three black kittens with mittens. Oh, no! One of the adorable kittens with mittens is missing!"

"Oh, my goodness!" said Grover. "I, Grover, will search high and low for the missing black kitty with mitties."

"Mew!" said the kittens.

"Here are Ernie and Bert at the duckie pond," said Grover. "Hello, Ernie! Hello, Bert! Have you perhaps seen a black kitty with mitties? He is missing."

"Why, no, I'm afraid we haven't seen any kitty," said Bert.

"Hi there, Grover," said Ernie.

"Quack, quack!" said the ducklings.

"Squeak, squeak!" squeaked Rubber Duckie.

"How did you know I was at the chicken coop?" asked Big Bird.

"Just lucky, I guess," answered Grover. "Have you seen a cute little black kitty with mitties?"

"No, Grover. Nobody here but us chickens! Here, chicky-chicks!" called Big Bird.

"Aha!" said Grover. "The chicks just hatched from those eggs. There is the mommy hen and there is the daddy rooster. They must be so proud!"

"Cock-a-doodle-doo!" crowed the rooster.

"Bawk!" clucked the hen.

"Cheep, cheep!" sang the chicks.

"Now, where is that kitty? Maybe the sweet little bunnies will know," said Grover. "Oh, you are so cute when you wiggle your noses. I will feed the bunnies some tasty carrots.

"This is my favorite bunny. Her name is Babbie Rabbit."

"Crunch, crunch!" said Babbie.

"Yoo-hoo, Herry Monster!" Grover called. "Is there a little black kitty with mitties anywhere in this field?"

"No, there are no kittens here," said Herry Monster. "Say hello to Maysie the cow and her calf Seymour."

"How do you do!" said Grover. "Moo!" said Maysie.

"And now for the barnyard," said Grover. "Look, there is the daddy gander. And there are the baby goslings. Look at them walking one by one behind the mommy goose."

"Honk!" said the goose and the gander.

"Honk, honk!" said the goslings.

"Honk, honk, honk!" honked the Honkers.

"Let us visit the pig pen now. Maybe the little kitty is here," said Grover.

"Furface," said Oscar, "kittens don't like mud. Pigs like mud because it's cool. And Grouches love mud because it's yucchy!"

"What adorable piggies," said Grover. "Did you know that a mommy pig is called a sow? Look at all the piglets running lickety-split to their mommy," he said. "She's telling her babies that it is time for lunch."

"Oink!" grunted the sow.

"Oink, oink!" squealed the piglets.

"Meet the sheep family," said Grover. "These are lambs. They are baby sheep."

"A daddy sheep is called a ram, and a mommy sheep is called a ewe," said Prairie Dawn.

"The lambs are so soft and woolly," said Grover. "Ooooh! Soft as a kitty. That reminds me, where is that kitty with mitties?"

"Baa, baa!" said the lambs.

"I hope the little black kitty with mitties is here at the paddock," said Grover. "Horses and donkeys play in the paddock. Baby horses and baby donkeys are called foals."

"No fooling," said Cookie Monster.

"Look at the foal running and kicking with his long and spindly legs," said Grover.

"Neigh!" said the horse.

"Neigh, neigh!" said the foal.

"Hee, haw!" said the donkeys.

"Caw, caw!" crowed the crow.

"Cowabunga!" said Cookie Monster.

"What a steep hill this is," said Grover. "I wish I could find the kitty with mitties up here! But it is worth the climb to meet the mommy goat and her babies, who are called kids.

"Pant, pant!" said Grover.

"Maaaaaaa!" said the goat.

"Maaaaaaa! Maaaaaaa!" said the kids.

"Have you seen an adorable black kitty with mitties up here in this tree?" asked Grover.

"No, Grover," said Betty Lou. "Only these baby robins. Look, but don't touch. The babies just hatched out of eggs."

"How sweet!" said Grover.

"Tweet!" sang the mommy bird.

"Tweet, tweet!" sang the baby birds.

"Oh, I am so tired!" said Grover. "I have just enough energy left to introduce you to the mommy dog and all her puppies. Oh, joy, there is the missing black kitty with mitties. You little scoundrel! You have probably been playing here with the puppy dogs all along."

"Woof!" barked the dog.

"Yip, yip!" yapped the puppies.

"Mew, mew!" meowed the kitten.

True or False?

Raccoons roast their corn before they eat it. True or false?

FALSE. But they do sometimes dunk their food in water before they eat it.

Penguins like to go sledding. True or false?

TRUE. They slide down snowy hills on their stomachs.

Elephants wear hats. True or false?

TRUE. Elephants sometimes make hats of wet grass and mud to keep the hot sun off their heads.

Whales sing to each other. True or false?

TRUE. They make sounds like singing which seem to "tell" things to other whales.

Bulls charge at a red cape because they hate red. True or false?

FALSE. Bulls are color-blind and can't tell red from any other color. Bulls charge at a cape waving in front of them because of its movement, not its color.

Gorillas like to play checkers and chess. True or false?

FALSE. But baby gorillas play games very much like follow the leader and king of the mountain.

Animals Under the Sea

Many animals live underwater.

seahorse

lobster

clam

starfish

squid

dolphin

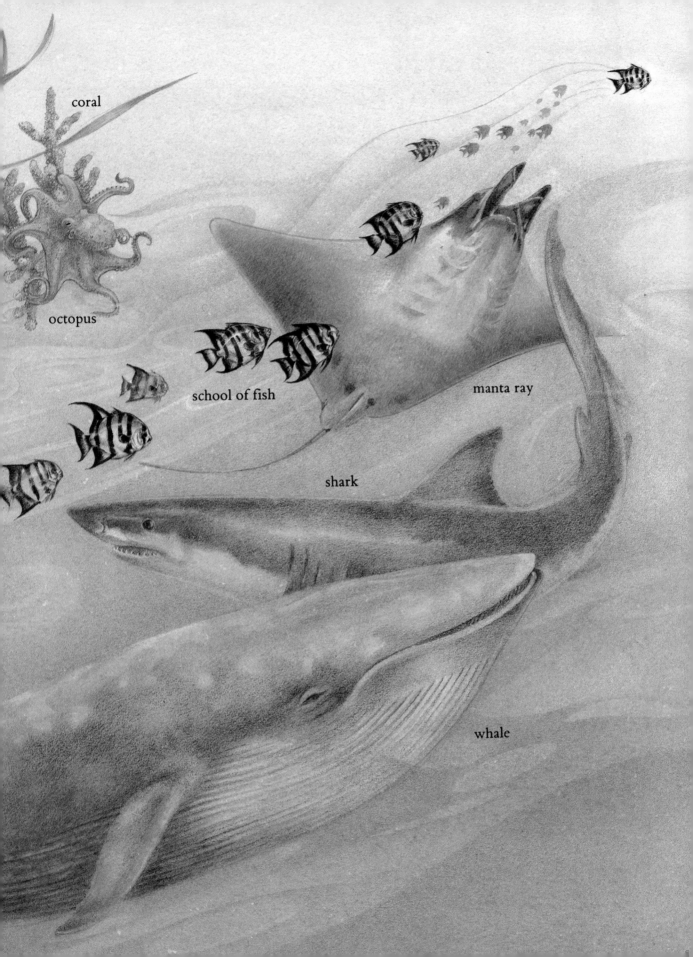

coral

octopus

school of fish

manta ray

shark

whale

Bert's Poem

"A bee's home is a hive.
A bird's home is a nest.
A squirrel goes home to its tree
When it wants to rest.
A spider spins a web.
An anthill is for ants.
And ladybugs live in my garden
With the flowers and the plants!"

Can you find eleven ladybugs hiding?

Show Me the Way to Go Home

Take the bird home to its nest.
Take the bee home to its hive.
Take the spider home to its web.

Oscar's Yucchy Questions

What does a camel do when it's grouchy?
It spits.

Why do pigs roll around in the mud?
To keep cool.

Do goats eat tin cans?
No, but they chew on them because they like the taste of the glue that holds the labels on the cans.

What does a skunk do when it's afraid?
It sprays a stinky mist toward its enemy.

How can you get rid of skunk smell?
Scrub anything skunky with tomato juice, soap, and water.

"Hey! Who wants to get rid of it?"

Grover's Book of
Cute Little Baby Animals

I can hardly wait to read
my new library book,
Cute Little Baby Animals.
Would you like to read it with me?
You would? Oh, I am so happy!

Baby cats are called kittens.
Kittens have soft fur and
sharp claws. When kittens are
happy, they purr.

Baby dogs are called puppies.
They love to run and play.
Kittens and puppies make
good pets.

The baby raccoon can
climb up into its home in
a hollow tree.

A baby rabbit is a bunny. It has long ears and a short fluffy tail.

A baby deer is called a fawn. A fawn's spotted coat helps it hide in the grass.

Oh, my goodness. They are so cute and furry!

A newborn horse is called a foal. Foals can run on their long, thin legs soon after they are born.

Many farmers raise ducks and chickens. Ducklings are baby ducks. They can swim and find food a few hours after they are born.

Chicks are baby
chickens. They are
covered with fluffy
yellow feathers
called down.

A baby cow is called a calf. Calves
often sleep in a barn on a bed of warm,
dry straw.

Baby lions are called cubs.
Lion cubs like to play.
They have very sharp teeth
and claws.

A baby elephant is called a calf. The mother elephant can use her trunk to guide her little calf along. Elephants can also use their trunks to drink water or pick up food.

That is the end of my book. But wait! Do not go away! I have one more cute little baby to show you!

Animals in the Desert

Rattlesnakes, lizards, rabbits, coyotes, and other animals live in the desert.

I love the desert. There are sooo many grains of sand to count....One billion one tiny grains of sand, one billion two tiny grains of sand....

Animals in the Jungle

A jungle is a warm, wet forest with many large trees. Elephants, monkeys, parrots, pythons, and other animals live in the jungle. There are more kinds of trees in the jungle than anywhere else on earth.

There are more insects in the jungle than anywhere else, too.

Big Bird's Trip to the Zoo

Big Bird is taking a picture of his favorite animal in the zoo.

rhinoceros

camel

deer

gorilla

moose

chimpanzee

kangaroos

lions

zebra

ostrich

THE TALLEST BIRD IN THE WORLD.

tiger

"Greetings! I am the Count. Let me introduce you to my wonderful, beautiful bats!"

Bats are the only animals besides birds and insects that can fly. Most bats fly at night and sleep all day, hanging by their feet in caves or other dark places.

How do bats fly at night without bumping into things?

Bats have a special kind of hearing which helps them sense where things are, even when they can't see them.

Are bats really blind?

No. Many people think that bats are blind, but they're not.

...Cats

"Here, kitty, kitty, kitty! I like pussycats because they have soft fur just like mine. Ya."

How can you tell if a cat is scared?

When a cat is frightened, it hisses, arches its back, and puffs up its fur.

Why do cats lick themselves?

To get clean. Cats lick themselves all over with their scratchy tongues to clean their fur. They wash their faces and their ears by licking their paws and using them as washcloths.

How do cats climb trees?

By digging their claws into the bark of the tree. Cats also use their claws as weapons.

Is it true that cats have nine lives?

No. People just say that because cats have a knack for getting out of danger.

Can cats see in the dark?

Cats are able to see in very dim light but not in complete darkness.

Sesame Street Pet Show

Can you name all the
pets in the pet show?
Which pet is the smallest?
Which pet is the biggest?
What animal would
you like as your pet?

BIGGEST

The Tail End

How do animals use their tails?

Beavers use their tails to pack down mud on their dams.

Beavers slap their tails on the water to warn other beavers of danger.

Kangaroos use their tails to push themselves off the ground when they jump.

Cows and horses use their
tails as flyswatters.

Opossums use their tails
to hang from branches.

Some monkeys swing from
tree branches by their tails.

Fish swim by pushing
themselves through the water
with their tails.

What's for Dinner?

Some snakes can unhinge their jaws to swallow an egg larger than the width of their bodies.

"What do Cookie Monsters really eat? Cuppy cakes. (And fruits and vegetables, and cheese and meat.)"

Pelicans catch fish for dinner.

An anteater sticks out his long tongue to lick up ants and other insects.

Cows and horses eat grass.

Flamingoes eat with their heads upside-down. They filter mud with their beaks to find tiny bugs.

Giraffes eat leaves from the tiptops of acacia trees.

How Do Animals Sleep?

"Time for sweet dreams."

Leopards sometimes sleep in trees.

A sloth sleeps hanging by its feet.

A pigeon sleeps with its head under one wing.

Some sharks lie on the bottom of the ocean when they sleep.

Owls sleep in the daytime.

A flamingo sleeps standing on one leg.

Horses sometimes sleep standing up.

Some animals sleep almost all winter. Bears, woodchucks, lizards, frogs, toads, turtles and some snakes take a long winter snooze.